# peg + cat

## The Eid al-Adha Adventure

JENNIFER OXLEY

+ BILLY ARONSON

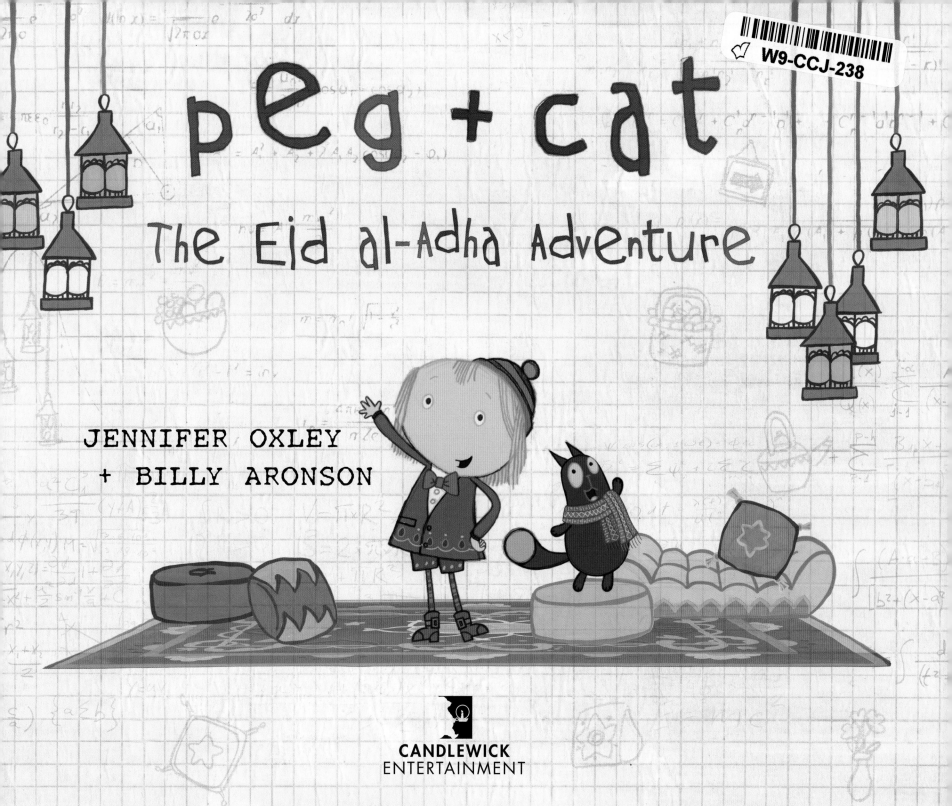

CANDLEWICK
ENTERTAINMENT

Peg and Cat were visiting their friends
Yasmina and Amir during a very special holiday.

2+1=3

It was Eid al-Adha, a holiday Yasmina and Amir celebrated every year. Peg and Cat had never even heard of Eid al-Adha until Yasmina and Amir invited them to the celebration to check it out.

"We're going to make your first Eid al-Adha the best ever," said Yasmina.

"Let's rock out!" said Amir.

They sang:

"Amir here,

And Yasmina the machine-a,

Rocking the house

Just like rockin' the arena!"

"Got my **new tie and jacket!**"
sang Amir.

"Got my **best hijab!**"
sang Yasmina.

"Got my **suit!** Cat has his **scarf** on!"
sang Peg.

"I'm **no slob!**"
sang Cat.

6+1=7

"Eid al-Adha is really fun," said Yasmina.
"There are presents.
And lots of food."

"But mostly," said Amir,
"it's about giving to those with less."

"I like the presents and food," said Cat.
"But giving stuff away? How is that fun?"

"You'll see," said Amir.

"Are those honey cakes?"
Cat asked.

"Should we add--"
Yasmina began.

**"MORE!"** said Cat.
**"MORE MORE MORE!"**

It was time to go to the celebration.

"Every year we bring this silver tray,"
Yasmina explained,
"filled with almonds, olives, apricots, and --"

"I love apricots!" said Peg.

"Then let's add **more,**" said Yasmina.

Amir played his stringed instrument, called
an oud. Yasmina played her electric guitar.
Peg and Cat played ukulele and drums
as their hosts sang about the holiday.

"*Eid Mubarak*

Means happy holiday!

So we say *Eid Mubarak*

As we celebrate.

On Eid al-Adha,

Even Cat is going to see

How awesome giving can be!"

"We'll see if I see!" said Cat.

10+1=11

"One important tradition," said Amir,
"is dividing the meat into three equal parts."

"When you have three equal parts of something,
each part is a **third,"**
said Peg.

"We keep **one-third,"**
said Amir.
"We give **one-third**
to our neighbors,
and we give **one-third**
to someone with **less."**

**"Less** what?" asked Cat.

"Food or clothes -- the basic stuff
that everyone needs," said Peg.

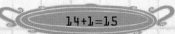

Amir divided the meatballs into three parts.

"Um, the three bowls all have
different amounts of meat, Amir," said Peg.

"But I put the same number of meatballs
in each bowl!" said Amir.

"The meatballs are different sizes though," said Peg.
"If we don't divide the meat into three equal parts,
this won't be the best Eid al-Adha ever!
# We've got a BIG PROBLEM!"

Peg noticed Cat playing with
a pair of small swinging pans.

"That's it!" she said. "The pan balance!"

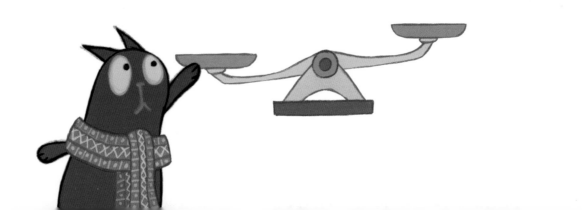

Peg put one pair of bowls on the pan balance.

"This pan goes down because the bowl on it
has more meat--it's heavier," she said.

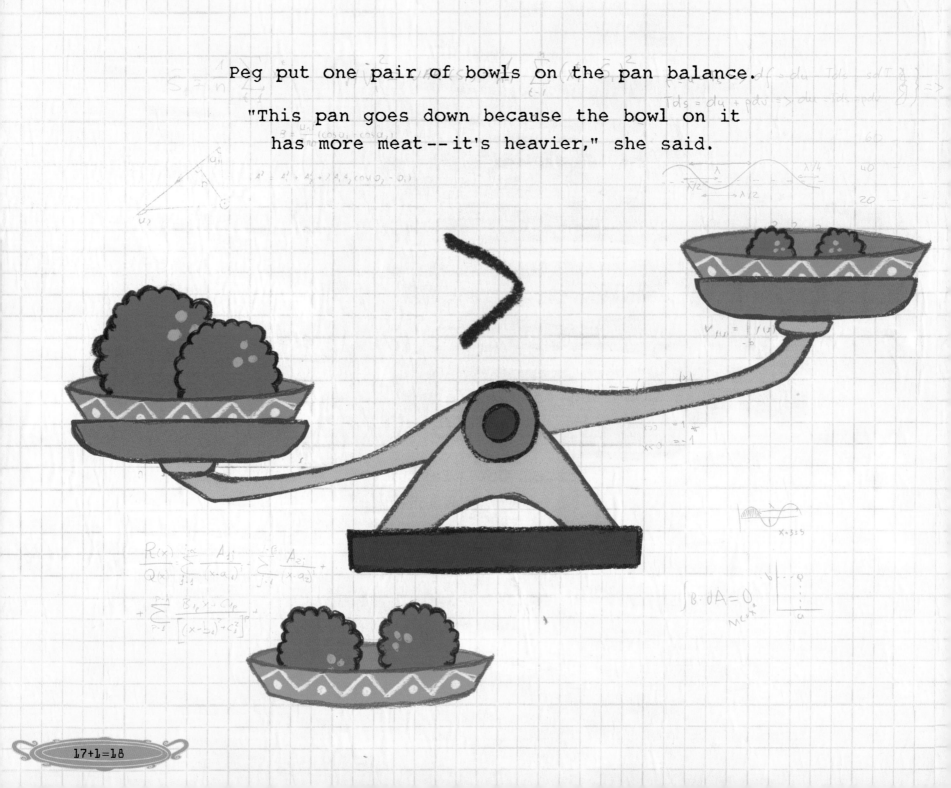

"But we can take from **more** and give to **less**,"
said Amir, "until..."

"The pans are at the same level!" said Yasmina.
"The meat in the bowls weighs the same!"

Peg replaced one bowl on the balance with the third bowl.
"These weigh the same, too! They all weigh the same!

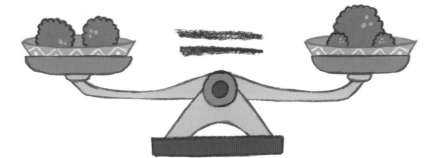

# Problem solved!"

## *"Eid Mubarak!"* said Cat.

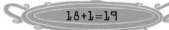

The group headed out for the party.
But first they had to drop off
**a third** of the meat to someone with less.

"We've come to the soup kitchen,
because the people who eat here have **less,"**
said Yasmina.
"At the soup kitchen they can get a good free meal."

As the door to the soup kitchen opened, Amir said,
"It's run by--"

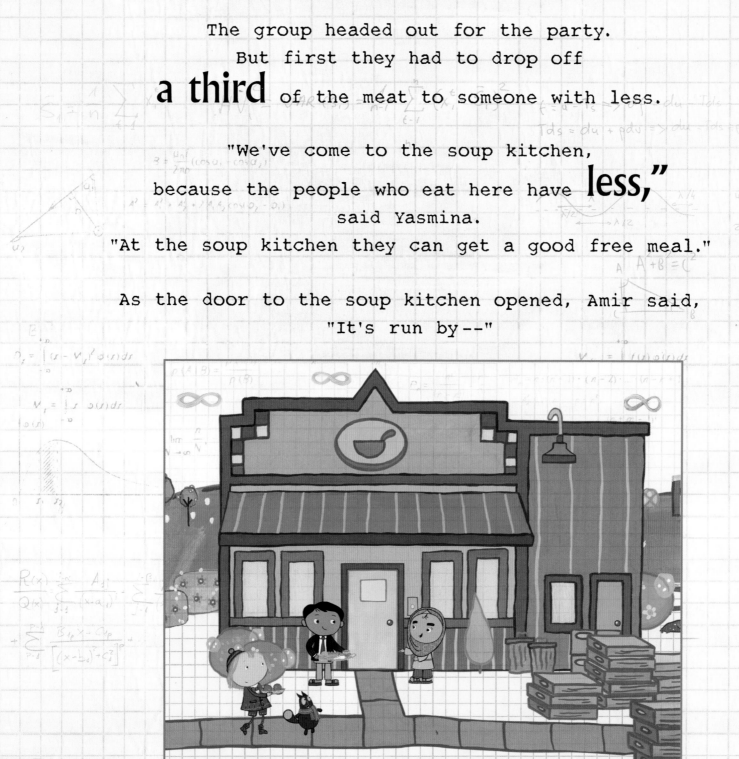

**"Ramone!"** said Peg.

Cat took the bowl from Peg and handed it to Ramone.
"We hate to run and eat,
but we have a party to go to," he said.

"Wait," said Ramone.
"I need your help with a

# REALLY BIG PROBLEM.

There's a man who lives
in that building across the yard.

He always comes here for meals.
But today he hasn't come.

I wonder if he's sick, or if those crates
of canned food that were just delivered
are blocking his way."

"Can't he order takeout?" asked Cat.

"NO," said Peg.
"Today's about giving.
We're going to give! We'll cross
the yard with the meatballs!"

The crates were piled so high,
Cat wondered how they would ever
get past them.

23+1=24

"Let's count the crates to find the piles with **less,**"
said Yasmina. "They'll be easier to step over."

"We can step across the piles with **less** with no stress!"
said Amir.

They stepped across a pile
that had only one crate
and another pile of two crates.

"One is **less** than six,"
said Peg.

"And ten is **more** than two!"
said Cat.

But there were even **more** crates
to get past!
Yasmina and Amir were

# TOTALLY FREAKING OUT!

"Cat's right," said Peg. "You should count backward to calm down."

"We'll count from seven," said Yasmina. "We like seven. Seven days
of the week, seven colors in the rainbow..."

7 6 5 4 3 2 1

As they counted, Cat gazed at those juicy meatballs.
He was about to take a bite when Peg shouted,
"That's it, you meatball-loving Cat! We'll divide the crates into thirds,
just like we did with the meatballs. They'll be easier to move.

# Problem solved!"

26+1=27

When Peg knocked on the door,
she heard a familiar voice invite them in.

"Mac?" asked Peg.

"I've had some bad luck," Mac explained.
"I usually go to Ramone's soup kitchen for food.
Last night I stubbed my toe, and this morning
I stubbed another toe. I'm not going anyplace."

"You don't have to," said Yasmina.
"We brought you meatballs!"

27+1=28

Mac was so hungry that
he ate the meatballs quickly.
For dessert, Amir and Peg offered him
olives and apricots.

Cat wanted to keep the honey cakes
for himself. But he remembered
that Eid al-Adha is about
giving to those with less.
So he took the tray over to Mac.

28+1=29

This book is based on the TV series *Peg + Cat*.
*Peg + Cat* is produced by The Fred Rogers Company.
Created by Jennifer Oxley and Billy Aronson.
*The Eid al-Adha Adventure* is based on a television script
written by Billy Aronson and background art by Erica Kepler.
Art assets assembled by Sarika Matthew.
Advisors Khalid Latif and Mazaher Tejani contributed to the
television episode upon which this book was based.
The PBS KIDS logo is a registered mark of the
Public Broadcasting Service and is used with permission.

pbskids.org/peg

First paperback edition 2019

Library of Congress Catalog Card Number 2018946151
ISBN 978-0-7636-9932-1 (hardcover)
ISBN 978-1-5362-0680-7 (paperback)

19 20 21 22 23 24 APS 10 9 8 7 6 5 4 3 2

Printed in Humen, Dongguan, China

This book was typeset in OPTITypewriter.
The illustrations were created digitally.

Candlewick Entertainment
an imprint of Candlewick Press
99 Dover Street
Somerville, Massachusetts 02144

visit us at www.candlewick.com

Scan this QR code with your smartphone or tablet
to watch a clip of the song "Eid Mubarak!" from *Peg + Cat*!

"Would you like a honey cake?"
Cat asked.

"I love honey cake!" said Mac.

Cat gasped. "Hey, giving *does* feel good!"

"You're all so nice!" said Mac.
"I don't know what to say."

"I do," said Peg. *"Eid Mubarak!"*

# EID MUBARAK!